Ella's Bear Wears a Hat of Air

Valerie Jaeger

Illustrator: Kyle Completo

Ella's Bear Wears a Hat of Air
Copyright © 2023 by Valerie Jaeger

All rights reserved. No part of this publication may be reproduced, distributed, or transmitted in any form or by any means, including photocopying, recording, or other electronic or mechanical methods, without the prior written permission of the author, except in the case of brief quotations embodied in critical reviews and certain other non-commercial uses permitted by copyright law.

Tellwell Talent
www.tellwell.ca

ISBN
978-1-998190-86-7 (Hardcover)
978-1-998190-85-0 (Paperback)

To Jordyn, Graeme, and Bentyn
who know that bears wear air and who
taught me how to be a Nonna

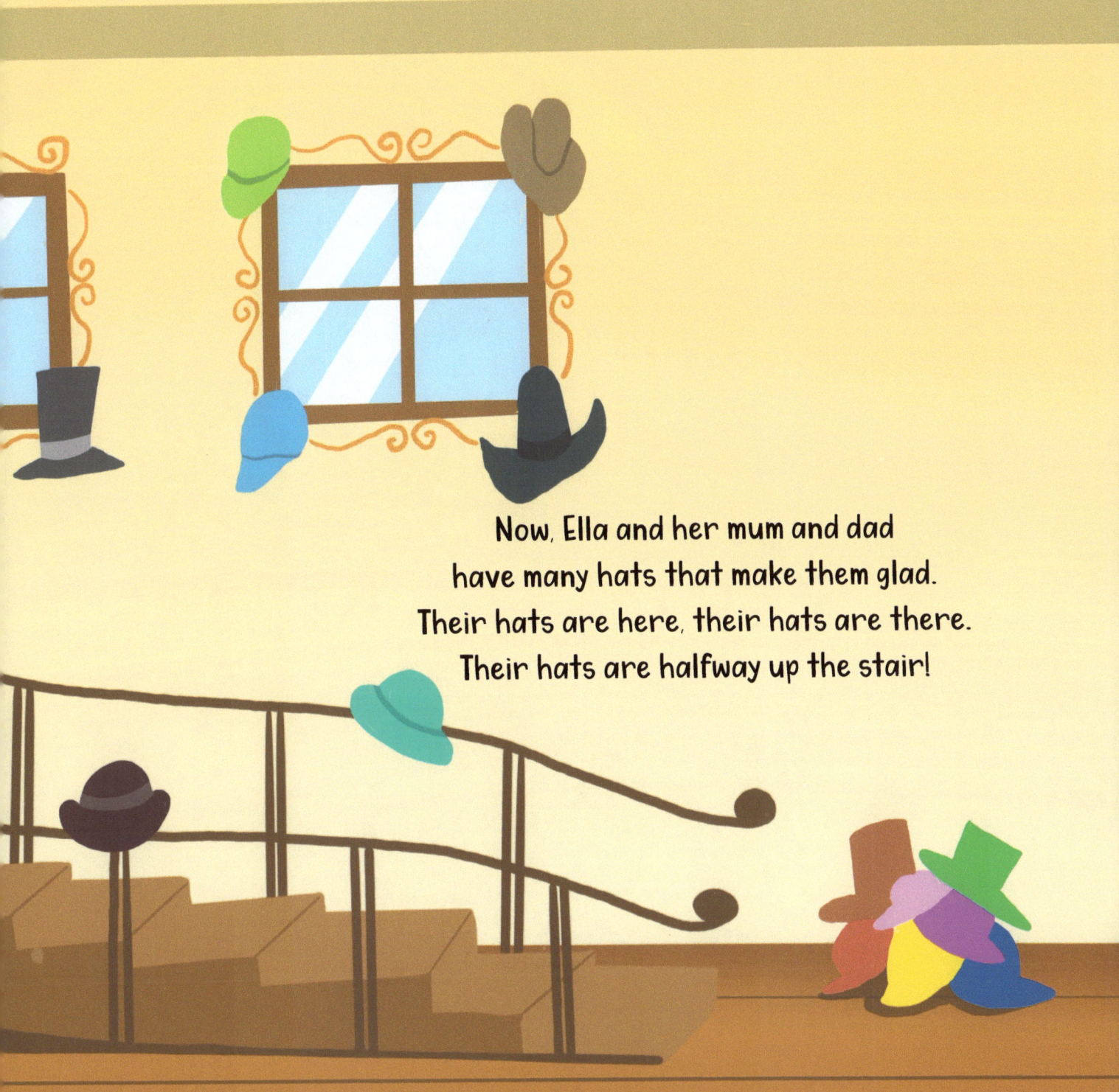

Now, Ella and her mum and dad
have many hats that make them glad.
Their hats are here, their hats are there.
Their hats are halfway up the stair!

But hats can take up so much space.
They had to build a separate place!
With special hats for work and play,
and different hats to match each day.

A yellow hat for when it's hot.
A blue fleece cap for when it's not.
The pink one works for picking berries.
The red hat helps for eating cherries.

But Ella needed just one thing.
A little friend to share her swing.
Mum and Dad have got each other.
Who's my sister or my brother?

One day when climbing very high,
a snuffling bear she did espy.
He wandered in and made her smile.
They ran and jumped and skipped a while.

And Ella knew right then and there
that even with his coarse brown hair,
the bear was just the one to be
a member of her fam-i-ly.

So off she went to ask her mum
if Bruno bear could be her chum.
But Mum and Dad were of one mind.
That Ella's bear was not their kind!

"We do not mind the big, black claws.
We do not mind his gaping jaws.
And even though he's very big
that would not bother us a fig."

"The problem, plain as day, is that
he never, ever wears a hat.
So, he cannot be your brother.
Go look again and find another."

Now, Ella really liked her bear.
Her toys and games they both would share.
Together they could head to Mars,
or zoom around in little cars.

Yet everything they did and said,
had one small hat and one bare head.
And Ella knew this would not do.
The heads with hats should count to two.

So, every day while up in trees,
or in the yard she'd ask him, "Please!
Just wear a hat and be like me.
Then you can join my fam-i-ly!"

She tried not seven, not eight, but NINE.
There must be one he'd think just fine!
He shook off each and calmly said,
"I'd rather wear the air instead."

Now, Ella came to realize
that you must look with brand new eyes
to see what always has been there.
The hat on the bear is the air!

His hat is mighty, big, and wide.
It stretched for miles from side to side.
His hat is very, very tall,
but made from atoms so, so small.

She ran and ran to find her folks
as they raked leaves beneath their oaks.
She tried and tried with all her might
to make the words come out just right.

"Instead of making all the fuss
to make the bear be just like us.
Oh, Mum and Dad, please come and see.
Please come and you'll agree with me."

"He has a hat upon his head.
It can be blue or black or red!
And we can wear it if we try—
it is the big, wide open sky."

Both Dad and Mum sat down to think
with thinking caps in blue and pink.
When they were done, they did declare,
"It's time we tried to wear the air."

To feel the air just might be nice,
unless the day is cold as ice.
To feel the air just might be fun,
unless your face gets too much sun.

Together on a log four sat,
With sunset sky as their new hat.
"When sky is changing blue to red,
we'd rather wear the air" they said.

About the Author

Valerie Jaeger is a physician and a grandmother who lives on Vancouver Island where the trees are very big. Her life's work has taught her that to truly celebrate diversity sometimes it helps to find some common ground.

Printed in the USA
CPSIA information can be obtained
at www.ICGtesting.com
JSHW041914081223
52977JS00006B/22